Calm from the chaos

Calm from the chaos

About the author

Keith David Burton was born in Bedford North wing hospital on January 13th, 1965. Raised by working class parents he was the youngest of five children on a council estate in Goldington.

Burton currently resides in the local town centre where he finds inspiration through his observations in and around the town, it's people and the many green spaces surrounding it.

A keen coarse angler for much of his life, Burton gained a first-hand insight of the natural world through his adventures on the great river Ouse and local lakes and fisheries in and around Bedfordshire.

This can often be seen reflected in many of his works. Like many artists, Burton has been at his most prolific during adverse periods in his life.

This is Burton's second and follow up poetry collection following his 2021 debut poetry collection -Through porcelain glasses. More of the same, this book continues to be inspirational writings based on influences from his own struggle with mental health, addiction and relationships.

The book demonstrates Burton's traditional style, encompassing deep imagery, rhyme, flow, metaphor and wordplay. Various facets of poetry are utilised, particularly his fondness towards micro poetry.

You can also follow Keith's latest work on instagram...

@Kb_poetry_emotion

All original content including cover photography by Keith Burton except for the following collaborations

*Keith Burton & Jaime Boey @jaimeboey

**Keith Burton & Denise Rusley @nobullheart

***Keith Burton & Sharvari Patil @lostworldwordss

****Keith Burton & Chaimae Saoud @myworld_yourhope

Cover art by Jah- DNA

Warning: contains some explicit material

Calm from the chaos

Content

Calm from the chaos

A calm exterior
Hidden with due diligence
Behind a second skin
A cupboard full of skeletons

The chaos within
Betrayed by lying smiles
Protecting every sin
Every once in a while.

Second chances

Melting a mountainous candle
An internal inferno of torture
Slow cooker on the back burner
Sadistic selfish debaucher

Driving the vehicle of destiny
Father Time without his glasses
Swerving an entire lifeline
Overtaken by second chances.

Frozen

The hands of time
A myriad of thoughts
Captured slowly
Memories caught.
Frozen on ice
Stored in the deep freeze
Defrosting fast
Thawing seas.

Great

Queendom of freedom

Majestical region

Magnetic cohesion.

Kingdom sensational

Diverse multi racial

Population palatial.

Our song

The first time our eyes met
That glowing dance
That first kiss
Creating romance.

Those initial feelings
Magical and strong
From that moment we knew
This would be our song.

She Devil

She is not on the level
Deep down in her own world
Inflamed with much ill feeling
Firing off underground

She makes me come alive
When almost at deaths door
My tongue twisted heathen
Licks me to the floor

She Devil whom I worship
She keeps me on my toes
A wildfire from hell
Spreading warmth wherever she goes.

Class Z

A tiny handful
High maintenance smile
Spoon-fed and watered
Half-naked defiance.

Trash strapped for cash
On bended knee
Getting down and dirty
Miss Trifle of sleaze.

Crocodile tears

Those alligator eyes
Turn on the waterworks
Crocodile tear in disguise
Once bitten twice shy
Too often I've swallowed her lies.

She swamps me underfoot
Feels like I'm running in water
In quicksand gripping slow motion
Beneath jaws a final death roll
I'm drip fed into her ocean.

Sonnet of silence

A solitary test
Confinement serves him best
No diversion distraction
Just self-control inactive

Cowering in the dark
Depression hitting hard
Punch drunk by anxiety
Floored silently

An indictment in dismay
Personality ghost affray
No court in the land
No judge to understand.

Locked within his mind
No key no light no kind!

No room in hell

Artistically

Majestic stance

Rhythmic worlds collide

In time instep aligned

Dance!

Back-to-back

Virgin on prostitution
Complicated absolution
Contusions of the brain
Chastity and whore insane

Demanding quite immoral
Fuck then drown one's sorrows
Commanded to comply
The choice to laugh or cry

Rest on wicked laurels
As they beg steal and borrow
Both extortionately high
Kiss the best good buy.

Moonstruck

Meteoric flame
Orbiting the world
Oscillating wildly
Neon based silence
Spinning Luna girl.
Tranquillity be he
Radiation hides her smile
Uniquely proportioned
Crashing with precision
Kick-ass projectile.

Soulmates

So hungry for love
His bones are showing
Starving to death
Loneliness knowing

Incessant nothingness
Craves a good meal
Looking malnourished
Needs food to feel

Energy is waning
Weak for real warmth
Tired of snacking
His heart is informed

Cold weather pending
At tethers end
An Eleventh-hour knock
From a long-lost friend

Laying down to die
Given up all will
Dinner for two
Attending the ill.

Jeopardy

Double trouble
Twinning ladies
Impregnated
Having babies

Man on the move
Man on the moon
Maintenance fees
Coming soon.

Simple

Easy on the ear
Rolls off the tongue
Up in the air
Since time begun

Love, love, love
Three simple words
Complicated to achieve
Sounds absurd.

Conscious

In my mind I am free
In my heart I am broken
In my soul undefined
In my conscious I have awoken.

Shariah

Blue moon mood
Bohemian loose fit
Cerulean nude
Cleave the pink bits

Path to a watering hole
Laugh as the crow flies
Duped rather dubious
Gone to paradise

Force a horse to drink
For no extra charge
A canal so shire
Tows an unfair barge

In it up to the eyes
Azure manmade stream
This land of milk and honey
The watery wettest dream.

The chase

Ambiguous left open to interpretation
Delphic conversation profanity inane
Without rhyme or reason or explanation
Everything turning insane.

Sea sure

Wave upon wave
Lapping the shore
Dancing with ease
Ebbing no more

Flowing with poise
Growing on me
Beautiful view
Picturesque she.

The early bird

Bookworm with a drink problem
Wriggling between the lines
Reading from cover to cover
An affliction unbenign

Recovering to discover
Her rocky path of pages
Sundried on the tarmac
Quite parched and vacant

Drying out down and out
Supping by the bridge
No silence in her library
His violence but a glitch.

Militia

Crackhead with a conscience
Hung out and left to dry
Hanging in the balance
Trust issues in disguise

Occupational hazard
Dying for bad habits
Last in the queue
Yet first to grab it

"OMG! This, that and the other"
Phone jacking drama queen
Nowhere left to hide
Downright disgusting

Chaos in a skirt
Living on the edge
One of her five a day
I don't mean 'fruit n veg'

Terrorist funded
All for her cause
Protesting loudly
Whilst on all fours.

Time

Minutes turn to hours
The passing of time
Inexplicable clockwork
Idle hands don’t chime

Crime paid with years
Tears behind the door
The longest of days
Slowly spent for sure

Time gulps each drink
As old age takes its grip
There's no looking back
No spare second left to sip.

X-ray eyes

Restoring the balance
Delicately poised
Grace and majesty
The pitch of her voice

An Irish Garden
Seen by the sea
Her position to bargain
Penetrating me.

Possession

Running rings around him
Her angel wings shatter
A metamorphosis
Fresh hooves pitter patter

She's fallen too fast
A lost soul possessed
Hoping for the worst
Expecting she's undressed

Exorcism of precision
She tries to repel
With fire in her eyes
He catches all hell

In a snatching last grasp
She gasps cleaner air
Adding light to her dark
See her wings reappear.

Blue Lune

Melancholy madness
Subdued sadness
Blue be thy name,
Dark is her heart
Deep like the stars
My Luna moon dame.

Shame cloud

Casablanca station
Depression taking aim
Running low on patience
Someone hides her pain

A thousand miles apart
She calls time every time
A shot to the heart
Pretending all is fine.

Cycles

Indolent moments
Lazing in the sun
Incoherent conversations
Shared with only one

Cycles of inactivity
Idly exchanged
Time zone indifference
Tandemly explained

Cozy separation
Prostrating overseas
No misinterpretation
Just let it be.

Slip sliding

Locked in a sanctuary
Escaping reality
Getting from A to B
It's all the same to me

Throwing away my soul
Diving deep up a hole
Going down without parole
A broken ladder beyond control

Splintered rungs snapped in half
Bleeding feet wrapped in scarves
Blistered hands slipping fast
My brainwashed smile's bloodbath.

Chaos crazy

Fallen in love with a tornado
Temptation I can't resist
Wrapped around her finger
thrown hand over fist

A gale force wind so brutal
Blows me in each and every way
Kissed by whirlwind beauty
Uplifting my stillest day.

Ocean eyes

Dark blue
Without surprise
Dazzling deep
Ocean eyes

Staring shared
A love so pure
Sea salt taste
Her bed assured

So untrue
Her mermaid lies
No eye contacts
Binding thighs.

Up in smoke

Drifting from home to home
Destination alone
Whenever she lays down
Her spirit freely roams

So full of bad habits
A long way past fun
Her addiction masses conviction
Sincere to everyone.

My sleeping beauty

My sleeping beauty
Timorously pirouettes
With aurora performance
Eloquently fouettés

Appealing allure
A fetching distraction
Ballerina dreamer
Inviting seduction

Expressive desire
An intriguing find
My sleeping dancer
Stimulating minds.

Curve ball

Curves in the right places
Curbing the tide
Fitting in spaces
Scarcely alive

Wishing he was here
Watching her back
Vulnerable seashell
See how she cracks.

Limbo

Left broken hearted
Since she's departed
He's lost for sure
Nobody to endure

Unanswered calls
Leave him appalled
Done nothing wrong
Yet she's just gone

Taken for a ride
Still on the slide
Emptiness sits
Replacing her bits

Thought they were friends

She's chose the end

Missing every breath

More energy in death.

Nowhere to turn

Free falling
Skin crawling
Relentless heartache.
Waves tidal
Goodbye's cruel
Suicidal case.

Puddles of love

Listening to every raindrop
Land between my heartbeat
Splash back on my dry eyes
Way beyond my wet feet
Deeper than alone street

Wishing for ifs, buts and maybes
Our paths crossing too soon
Puddles in every step taken
Reflections of my blue moon
No shelter from this sad tune.

Heartache

Arteries of the blood
Paths to ruby roads
Baths awash with memories
Steeping heavy loads

Thoroughfares from the heart
Pulsating around his world
Unexcavated secrets
Too deep to be told.

Death sentence

When you know you're out of time
They're the best days of your life
That clock just keeps on ticking
A strange calm without strife

Your affairs all in order
Matter of fact from then on
Goodbyes all said and done
No loose ends and your gone!

The secret garden

Beyond the iron curtain
Behind the windswept gates
Some wild and wintry wilderness
Stammers then hesitates

Amidst dark bower and glade
Shades of discontent
For who owns the padlock of time
Permanence be temporarily lent.

Insecurity

Shes too hot
It leaves him cold
Wasting his time
Or so he’s told

Wherever she heads
Everybody tails
Naked on heat
He’s dressed to fail

When she's away
The sun goes in
When she returns
The ice grows thin

She shines all day
A most radiant thing
Clouds gathering
Stop him melting.

Autumn child

She undresses in the dark
A bark worse than her bite
The winds of change start caressing
By gently teasing before daylight

Her summer attire cast asunder
Strewn across the bedroom floor
Thrown down with gay abandon
Discarded splendour worn no more.

Stripped to the core nervously exposed
A trembling statue blindly concealed
Standing naked ready for her show
Come dawn Miss Fall be revealed

With disruption comes destruction
She lays down her proud spoils
A brief picture of madness
Since she's gone off the boil

Such a deep-rooted sadness
Be robust and steadfast
For one moment in season
She removes her dark mask.

Metamorphosis

I cannot find the queen of butterflies
She loves landing on so many flowers
And flutters the prettiest of wings
I guess I'll never know where she's been
She comes and goes
The wind blows her off course
Onto the richest of kings.

Perpetual pain

You have left me hanging
See how I linger
Anticipating my fate
Like a witch's curse
My blood on your fingers

I would jump if I could
But it would be in poor taste
Going out of my mind
Running out of time
To a much better place.

Mermaid man

Scratch under the surface
Holding onto his breath
Like a fish out of water
He’s flirting with death

He sleeps on his own
Upon her coral bed
His wet infatuation
Deep down giving head.

Hard work

Building blocks of hope
Stacking in her favour
Sky high ambition
Without the hard labour

No short cuts to a fortune
Her world will tumble down
Dreams full of half measures
Come crashing to the ground.

Bewitched

Possession obsessing most grippingly
Digging her claws into me
Tearing me apart from myself
Sharing me with just herself

Under her spell most obviously
Bewitched and bewildered naturally
In shackles quite unashamedly
This ball and chain's amazing (she)

Mist

Same eerie sense of density
Some epiphany implodes beneath
An ill feeling bitter eyes are following
Haunting paranoia without relief
My red mist and visionary thief.

Taking off

When love perched on my windowsill
Still flapping her broken wings
Her sad lament sung beautifully
A serenade befitting kings

New lovebirds thus fused together
Healing hearts and fulfilling goals
Growing stronger in every way
Cementing hope two concrete souls.

Masterful

Sharing marshmallow kisses
Fluffy pillow puckered lips
Sweet soft empowered
Remote controlled fingertips.

Stroking her brow
Gently combing her hair
Blowing breaths in her ear
Enslaved by her stare.

Real life

Fickle friends fade away from the world of love
Dispensing a million memories once they've seen enough
The fragile silhouette of happiness strains hard to crack a smile
Rarely seen in the here and now disappearing all the while.

The art of time

A sharp knife forsakes the air
Causing the tallest tree to tremble
Despite no ill wind and clear skies above
Like an arctic blue shade by pencil

The rush hour stumbles in due haste
Tripping over slippery feet
Smooth pavements tired of being walked on
No oil painting, these tarnished streets

Wet footsteps, dampening sand
Striding wide stretching worlds
One nervous couple feign true love
Transparent yet quietly loud

Harmony holds up her hands in disarray
Humility buries his head underground
Fight or flight nobody cares
Pessimism is all around

Optimism beckons the clouds of time
As dry footprints fall back to grain
Clinging in hope to both souls
Dying out until the rain.

Veil of comfort

Every shade of black
Worn with a dark background
Unashamedly trying to hide
Not wanting to be found

Ebony stands beside me
My shyness crutch and friend
I lean on her shadow
Hoping the night don't end.

Anonymous

Decanting high pressure
My corkscrew undoes
Exuding champagne class
Oozing from above

As pretty bubbles in a glass
She loves to come on top
Lavishly overflowing
Reluctant to stop

Spilt vintage fine wine
Stains just the same
He peels off the label
Never knowing her name.

Virgin island

Sugar coated white lies
Leave crystal clear steamy lips
With nothing whispered sweet
He tames her wild hips

Tethered by dark forces
Shackled to wet skin
She bends over backwards
For her first taste of sin.

War and peace

Silence

Peacetime smiles

Remembering vile war

Fast forward past hostile

Violence!

French miss

With cold blooded ease
She scores his thin skin
Chic surgical precision
Her scalpels are in

With a vice like grip
She concludes her attack
Sharp Parisian guillotines
Finishing off in the sack

Nailed to every corner
Of some four-poster bed
The blood on her hands
Only in his head.

Happy ever after

Far and away over the honeymoon
Where intimate stars no longer shine
A duet of speechless flowers passing bloom
Waste many hours counting time
And the fewest of times spent in one room
No heart and soul my bride and groom
Unlike two broken bookends
No happy ending happened too soon.

On the edge

Walking in the long grass
Frisking thickets and sifting sedges
Looking for a reason
Grazing knees clambering trees
Drinking to remember

Lost my way somewhere near
Please leave me alone
With frost bitten fears
A waterfall of tears
In the darkness of November

No birds and bees

Or pleasurable sneeze

I'm tripping on drowning leaves

Soake the bone

By Autumns dying embers.

Time stood still

Creeping ivy slinking slyly climbing trees
Shes behind me thinking blindly I can’t see
Hiding shyly aiming highly the hands of time
Edging nearer I can feel her hands on mine.

Venus's flytrap

Windswept blushes sweeping childlike crushes
Blowing his mind
Handpicked cherries hide poisonous berries
Temptations so unkind

Mother Nature's babies intoxicating ladies
Blinding his sore eyes
Harvested to savour the fruits of hard labour
She’s opening her thighs

Venus traps her fly rolling over to die
Still seeing stars
He crawls back to Mars!

Angel of the east

An angel has caught a cold
And sneezes from the east
A blizzard of spider leaves
Spin a web of dreams
Then cast it over me.

Battleground

Her brittle candy floss defences
Break up his place of worship
Shattered stain glass windows
Litter cathedrals without mercy

A choir singing on the sidewalk
Choke back tears of ruin
Brave barbed wire voices
Reverberate so moving

Acoustics bounce off crumbling walls
Like cannon balls in slow motion
A fragile fairground attraction
His carousel of destruction.

White picket purgatory

White lines wrong time what lies behind
Take no notice of the fence
Outside smiles hide inside upheaval
Continuous sick pretence

Purgatory evil child abuse
Paedophile palaces burn in hell
Wicked picket entrapping minors
Hansel and Gretel's kiss and tell.

The luck of the Irish

Her horse drawn caravan
A shamrock and rolling gypsy
Full on superstition
No four-leaf clover
No rabbit's paw
Fuck off Friday the 13th
And your spear of destiny.
Not much indecision
He puts her on both knees
Her will is stolen
Pegged down
His fortune up
No lucky heather sir
No crystal ball necessary.

A winter tale

When short days adorn longer nights
Wearing the blackest of shadow
Winter bites down on autumn's tail
Trailing a bad taste in the mouth
November pales fond memories of pain
Bailing dark burning desire
Approaching December spilling daylight
Frost bitten laced embers on fire.

Samara

A sycamore leaves
Hopelessly falling she smiles
Quite random yet purposed
With twizzled penetration
Bequeathing mother nature's free ride

From a sycamore tree
Momentum is gathering pace
Compelling wing spreading
She glides down gently
Crash landing with such grace

A sycamore bleeds
So out of her tree she cries
Propelling dehydrated
Terminated but elated
No need to kiss her goodbye.

Sink or swim

Skimming shards of black slate
Water-skiing kissing surf
tragic swallows chasing shadows
Swoop into steppingstones
Nose diving sinking fast

Trying hard to make love
Ebbed pebbles on the beach
Mirrored liquid trickery
Conjured by the moonlight
Dying cheek to cheek.

When

When the sky is cleaved
Then the stars will scatter
When mountains crumble
And the granite shatters

When oceans surge
Then rivers may flood
and tears keep flowing
Drowning true love

When there is no island
And nowhere to hide
Then heartache be eternal
When two worlds collide.

Victoria's ashes

The aroma of welted leather
Walks out the tannery gates
Breathing in the smelted ore
Hammered for Victorian gain

Pennies a long way from heaven
Darn pockets of tattered holes
A starving matchbox peddler
Strikes out at a smoker's nose

A rag and bone's trusty steed
depositing excess hay
Where spilling jugs and bottles
Splash down with gross decay

Beer Swilling embellished stories
Are exchanged with drunken cheer
To the ladies of the night
While sharing gonorrhoea

Some baker's bread is cooling
Tantalising a pitiful boy's poise
The streets of London still echo
Perfumes of an artful noise.

Poetry devotion

Kiss me like poetry
Cover me in lip gloss glory
Tongue my tonsils senseless
Do it again and again
A happy ever after story.

Seeing stars

Lifes hard and then you die
Shooting stars leave darkening skies
Paradise awaits an angel
As heavenly tears fill my eyes.

The slippery slope

Downhill ride

On the slide to hell

Breaking up

Falling out

Roller-coaster roundabout

Underground farewell.

Nightlife

As a solitary nightingale sweetly sings
An owl spreads her hungry wings
A shaded hue hides one dark misnomer
She captures her prey by nocturnal aroma

A roost of pipistrelles navigate the waves
Devouring with precision flying beasties craved
Despite miniscule bloodshed and bodies torn
The land be pristine cometh the dawn

Time heals

Flushed by fresh betrayal
Whilst trying to hide one's face
Facing utter humiliation
Blushing is but a waste

The dark void left by lost love
Emptiness will doubtless replace
Believing better times shall consume
Eating away that bitter taste.

Life goes on

Everyone appears to have gone away
Not pulling no punches when I say
It hits much harder on New Year's Day.

If only

If only I could swap places with you
I would do it tomorrow
Not from self-pity
Nor out of sorrow

I wish you'd get better
You deserve much more time
On this imperfect planet
Where you are divine

You are so full of life
And I am dead wood
Not all bad news
Just misunderstood

So sweet and innocent
With no time on your side
Life has always been cruel
And now you have died.

Goodbye dearest

Goodbye to everyone you have ever known
Tomorrow never comes until you're all alone
Then you die slowly facing the unknown.

Hope

Adversity

Desperately coping

Tears drown choking

Still full of belief

Hoping!

Promises

Spoken

Meaningful words

Promises of integrity

Beautifully lied to me

Broken!

Breakable

Brittle porcelain angels
With pretty twists and tangles
Damaged delicate wings
Falling for my sins
Breakable heaven so fragile
Your rainbow be your smile.

Motherhood

Puts on a brave face
When she's dying inside
Smiling so broadly
While deep down she cries

With the weight of the world
Spanning across her shoulders
She never gives up
Carrying on like a soldier

Leaves her feelings till last
Doing all to please those
That hang off her back
As respect slowly goes

Shown every year
With a bouquet of flowers
Appreciation so rich
Given all her few hours

Shes finally at peace
Through the cemetery gate
And then the penny drops
When it's all too late.

Car crash

Chased by the devil
Chasing the dragon
The police on my tail
I've fell off the wagon

Running through lights
Red amber green
No chance of stopping
You know what I mean.

Believing

Somewhere between the sea and sky
My eyes start glossing over
I see beauty in every soul
Breathing out rainbows dipped in clover
Turning heads with smiles the world over.

Through my fingers

Ladies and gentlemen
Depression is a blessing
At least I feel pain
I'm not even messing

My so-called life
Is under house arrest
It brings out the worst in me
And it brings out the best

I don’t beat my chest
Aim my eyes at the ground
No lust to engage
No love to be found

Depressed is my guest
My companion full time
Alone with my destiny
Along with red wine.

Family tree

Shooting from the hip
Sick of climbing up words
Tired of listening
To the absolute absurd

The shit hits the fan
Yet again and again
Thank fuck for God
A (fucking) men

Life just gets worse
How much can I take
From my bloody family
For another mistake

Manipulation and lies
Are following my gaze
But from my blood
Spilt back in the day

This stick in the mud
Sinks into misery
The apple of my eyes
Too far from the tree

So close to home
A long way off course
Picking up my pieces
The splinters of divorce.

A long reach

Stimulated remote control
Her immersive imagination
A provocative voice
Penetrating her elation

Calm whispered simulation
Suggestively takes its toll
Repeated palpitations
Inflammatory on the whole.

Without a trace

Addiction diagnosed
Sanctioned or jailed
No one really cares
Either way I've failed

I who have nothing
Whatever no one sees
Much that don't come true
Especially my dreams.

Queen of arts

A tapestry for lovers
No metamorphic mosaic
Metaphor ignoring
One colossal ice thawing
Concealing all mistakes

A patchwork caterpillar
Picture perfect almost unheard
Where black and white can lie
And colourful butterflies do die
Painting majestic words.

Velvet on the mound

I feel your skin
Wonderfully magic
Youre steely grin
Suggestively tragic

A subtle touch
Peels you open
I'm in your head
Knowing youre hoping

I feel a deep velvet
Fingertipped and beguiled
Once in every blue moon
I come travelling miles.

Off balance

Contortions of the mind
She bends and she bows
The twist and turning kind
Flexibility unopposed

Gravitational forces
Are pulling him in
Dancing without her pole
A centrifugal sin.

Deadly symphonic

Like a violin concerto (well kind of)
Her tear-filled voice in E minor
Melancholy madness never ending
Reaching out inanely befriending
Apprehending hands from a dark cloud
Take him coveted in her shroud

He plays dead to avoid attention
Hoping for some divine intervention
Nothing heavenly to ease his plight
A Cadaver in plain sight
Hypnotized by relentless entertaining
That violin tames all complaining.

Tempestuous

The North wind ghosts her desert storm
She always blows hot and cold
A majestic force of nature
Invisibility I cannot hold

I beg the debris dancing in the breeze
Such graceful grains of sand
To parachute upon my stage
I hold my cup in hand.

Death innately

The sands of time take their time
Crippling to the core
One bad apple forever rotten
Withering on the floor

A slow death, one savoured breath
One second seems like four
Emerging today eroding away
Those sands of time no more!

Waiting

My angel of mercy is looking away
Blinded by countless hours counting pain
Although long gone, I sit here still hoping
Naïve optimism trumps thoughts of restarting
Chasms of anguish, voids surround my heart
Avoiding common sense, I stumble on art
I start staring at her last photograph
One reminiscent memory oh, how I made her laugh
Left perplexed and with no explanation
With not much choice, I continue creating
Without my angel, all feeling has gone for good
I commence reality, quite reluctantly as I should
Accepting the compensatory "just good friends"
Never to value a wasteful end!

Every wolf cries

Something hurts, then moving stirs
A fight ensues deep from within
The battle lost, it's just not to be
Control concedes to shy release.
Glistening trickles springing to clear
As puddled corners turn to tears.
Those eyes are not made to cry
When a grown man buries his head
Behind his hands to hide
Something inside him dies.

The one

A bouquet of beautiful smiles
Gift wrapped for paradise
Over seven seas to shine on him
Unlocking hearts without a key
Wide open arms never think twice

Decorating delights, no vase insight
Lighting up his darkening world
Prettier than any picture
awe-inspiring lip-read literature
Four billion flowers to find one girl.

Carrion

Stone the crows until Corvus tears
Blackened white noise spread wings in fear
As the crow flies, laughter dies clearly
Squawk filled silence replaced by tyranny
As crows cry.

Foggy

I try so hard to reach not preach
(We all know where that leads)
Feel me bleed in your hour of need
I'm sleeping with misdeeds
Sleepless!

Burning desire

Shes lost for good
In a forest fire full on dream
Climbing trees
Grazing her knees
Trying to smoke out
What it all means.

Treading on eggshells

A home built on sand
Life forever fragile
Risks taken daily
Confined in a prison.
What is hidden cannot hide
Swirling shells of precision
Survival as ever
Our primeval mission!

Buried treasure

In a secluded solitaire moment
Between dapple grey clouds
Beneath diamond dipped skies
A jewellery of liquid gold memories
Encrust salt sapphire eyes
Streaming until sunrise.

She is

She is the touch of my skin
The smile on my face
That spring in my step
My energy and pace

She is my darkest mood
The rage from within
My reason to live
My reason to sin

She is the tears in my eyes
Of a lost love unkind
The longing for happiness
I cannot find

She was my life
My every breath
She takes my last pulse
For she is death!

Never give up

The sun's not hiding
Rising up still out shining
On dark horizons.

We

What she will do for me
And what she does to me
My island all at sea
Stolen secret moments
Unique sweet components
Of intimacy.

Ye olde cold call

If thy like thou sound
ye welcome thee in
On thine contrary
Thou shalt do nothing

If thy door knock ignored be
Fear not thine guest
If ye doth oblige thee
Friend, thou art thy best!

Greener pastures

The tranquillity of green
At peace in these parts
Cloudless in mind
Calm and sedate times
Before all-out war starts!

Veiled threats

Dancing

Deadly nightshade

Sleepless black ballet

Lily of the valley

Blooming!

Deadlier than the male

He yields to her will
Like steel bends to fire
Kill or be killed
Swayed by desire
Tamed by a lion

He falls at her feet
Praying for predation
Rolling over completely
With wide eyed adoration
To utter domination.

The caged bird

Incarceration
Death row
Clipped wings flying
Time's pendulum is trying
Pardon!

Moon river

The Ides of march
Lamenting long
The fullest moon
Her Lycan tune
Howling on

Luna mood swings
Righting her wrongs
Is she barking mad?
Biting off the hand
That feeds her sad song
All hunger gone!

Snake charmer

Au revoir to his French kiss
Mam 'Selle of tasteful highs
No more forked tongue in cheek
Or slavering honeysuckle lips
Nor Boa constricting thighs

Slipping through his fingertips
Such unconvincing sighs
His snake in the grass venom
A tongue cut out for lies
Whispers her last goodbye.

Dead or alive

Death

Losing all

Bravely we fail

Downtrodden but standing tall

Breath!

Queen of darkness

Magically
Her majesty
Queen of dark
Wields her broken heart
Seductively!

Torture

Beautiful
Brutally thoughtless
Manipulative violent disorder
Illegally paid through extortion
Lawless!

Web of deceit

Tongue tied
Lost for words
Caught in her own net
Ironically
For her loose lips
Made such a mesh

Trapped beneath
Her web of deceit
For spilling lies
Spinning round
Now there's no sound
Her cobweb dies!

Clamming up

Encrusted
Pretty shell
Precious embedded pearl
Loving her oyster world
Embrace!

Anger management

They say the pen is mightier than the sword
You'd better believe it
You filthy fucking fraud
Forever scheming and dreaming
Stuffed full of semen
God! I must have been bored

Manipulation by masturbation
I'd sooner fuck Satan
His scorn less frequently poured
A pathological liar
Your stories so dire
And always ignored

A pocket psychotic
Highly strung and neurotic
How you made me squirm
Chain smoking while choking
Your cunt always soaking
Dripping with sperm

Way overrated
Your character berated
Your end is nigh
My pen's assassinated
My anger is sated
Now fuck off and die!

Paranoia

Paranoid delusions
Schizophrenic confusion
Polluting the mind
Sleep deprivation
Morbid fascination
Strange but kind

Manic deep depressive
Compulsively obsessive
So much strife
Grandiose beliefs
An imaginary thief
A stolen life

Managing such challenging
Chemically unbalancing
A brain insane
Psychotic must dos and déjà vu
Solitude I keep going through
It's happening again

Hallucinate love turns to hate
Everything seems down to fate
For all I know
Tortured moods that I import
Racing thoughts that I can't sort
Just won’t let go

Too many voices
White noisy choices
Leave me alone
Need a vacation
From medication
A place called home.

A woman scorned

Somewhere overlooking
With an eyeful of scorn
Boiling over black magic
Her spellbound telepathic
Cold yet strangely warm

Her dreams up in smoke
She lives she breathes she fires
No spark left of chemistry
Slow burning alchemy
Extinguishing desire.

Sacrifice

Sacrifice
For the greater good
Avoiding temptation
When no other could.

A beautiful mess

In heaven with the devil
Chasing dragons on cloud nine
Chaotic chasms be her master
Coming down given time

This angel looks like hell
As she stares into the sky
No diamond studded staircase
To help her get up high

At eternal war with herself
Lady Lucifer's mistakes
With ten thousand second chances
How many more will she make?

But will she ever break?
As she blows so hot then cold
Holding hands with her demons
While her heart is made of gold.

Needle in a haystack

Searching high and low
Casting out large and small
Scooping only thin air
Catching nothing at all

Fishing all seven seas
Trawling his big net
Hunting the thimble
Without success

In discovering her majesty
His royal cathedral
He pins all his hopes
To that one needle

Looked an entire lifetime
In too many haystacks
His soulmate is waiting
While he clutches at straws
She falls through the cracks.

Timeout

Absence abstaining
What are we gaining?
Does the heart grow fonder?
While we're complaining

Months of defiance
Avoiding violence
Despite the long distance
A stunning silence!

Sweet dreams

Transport your body to the vehicle of your mind
To a place travelled by our kind
Down a road somewhere only we go
To share secrets only we know.

Decided

Persistence

Moving forward

Never looking back

Once and for all

Distance!

Dead poets inside of me

Why do dead poets still crave to be?
Staring back at the future of opportunity
Weeping is the window reflecting bygone years
Tortured tempered glass deflecting happy tears

No quills shalt scribe the learned writers block again
Sheets of stacked up fables queueing in the rain
Sitting quietly oblivious weaving modern words
Inside the mind of destiny composing dated verse.

Sparks

Impulsive

Spontaneous seduction

Volcanic sexual chemistry

Explosive bang on ecstasy

Eruption!

Faith

When all rivers seem up in the air
When you've dived so deep to please
Where your beliefs drown in despair
Like wading on bended knees
Just keep swimming towards that estuary
Where the sky kisses the sea.

Tsunami

The oceans are seen drowning
In a sea far from tranquil
And the earth smiles screaming
As crescent moons jive and tango

The sky is on fire
While shooting stars dance in space
Clouds burn out in thin air
But nothing goes to waste.

No turning back

Drowning in reflections of the past
To bask in that playground called my youth
Cannot recapture precious moments, they never last
No dress rehearsal isn't that the truth!

Over my shoulder

When night is at its darkest before dawn
And you can't see the wood for the trees
When friendship so forlorn
And every sound fuels your unease

Somehow something keeps you going
But you just don't know what that is
An entity seemingly all knowing
Comes and calms every crisis.

High to low

Euphoria

Glorious feeling

What goes up

Must then come down

Grieving!

The tale of Mr Toad

This wee ode is about my friend
Mr Toad and his untimely end
One day he left his humble abode
(So many seeds to be sowed)
It sent him round the bend

His quarry lived just across the road
(He'd never read the green cross code)
Sufficiently mowed needless to say
Seeing him explode made my day

As for the culprit that drove the car
Some clueless chef who never went far
Hit and run was the said charge
Was no accident he remained at large

And for the lawman that let him off
As it so happens just loves his scoff
Invited him out for a free lunch
My only means to thank him a bunch

So much is owed to this unfortunate toad
(Just doing his duty to empty his load)
The legacy that he left behind
Is on my plate with a glass of red wine
"Toad in the hole" of a different kind!

Candlewicks

As bitterness bites another romance
Memories flicker like candlelight
Wax wanes and rains some more
Dripping in then out of sight.

Heartbreak takes healing hands
Scolding untold sands of time
Loving breezes of remembrance
Blows cuddles that cloud the mind.

The meaning of life

When you stop to ponder
And simply wonder why
Consider and contemplate
Why you live and die
Why you laugh and cry

When you give it too much thought
And think it makes no sense
That overwhelming question
Is it all a dream
Or something more immense.

Seeing stars

Life dies and then you're hard
Shooting stars in darkening skies
Paradise awaits an angel
As heavenly tears fill my eyes.

I wish I could

I wish I could write you a poem
I would read it every night by your bedside
I would fill every verse with wonder
Sweetly say how my heart grows fonder

I would sing it to you with music
Insist that you listened to my every word
I would say everything that I'm feeling
Mean the world to know I've been heard.

Ashes to ashes

Flaming ash tree matchsticks
Sparking fire
Ashtray remains
Smokers' funeral pyre.

Poetic ruins

In the good old days
Back in in the darkest age
Gothic scribblers scrolling away

Quilled feathers inspired
Before Ink fountains misfired
Blotting good verse per se

Archaeology revealed
this ancient art concealed
Poetic ruins still in tune today.

Ground zero

Ashes

Burning love

Lost all trust

Going up in smoke

Dust!

Hello again

Overgrown doorway

Found a new key to your heart

Opening up a fresh start.

Paper heart

In the palm of one hand
I was just torn apart
Ripped pieces of tissue
Broken bits of my heart

An unfolded creased sheet
Cannot reassemble its past
Like ironing crumpled paper
Lost trust can't be reversed.

She walked on water

She walks upon water
I ask my weeping eyes
There'll be no clouds in the sky
If she kisses me goodbye

I sigh beneath the sunset
And tumble towards the tide
In a wave of anticipation
loving before I die

She walked upon the water
I told my weeping eyes
Now there's only cloud
Where she kissed me goodbye.

Shut out

Overgrown doorway
Found a new key to your heart
Opening up a fresh start.

Loner

Obtuse without pretence
Morose
Insensitive and gross
Obsessing at its best

Objecting to everything
Cantankerous and sanctimonious
Somewhat ceremonial
But never on the fence

Anxious
Reluctance in abundance
Uprightness redundant
Overtly intense

Hidden deep inside

Substance abuse

Finally working loose

Recluse.

Shadows

Untouchable

Unflinching passion

No hard feelings

Feeding off sunlit rations

Shadows!

For pity's sake

I live my life like an apology
Forgive me for I have sinned
I'm sorry you ever met me
Oh, brother where do I begin

Wish I could turn back time
Another path I would choose
Oh, brother I implore thee
Spend one day in my shoes

Repentant five times a day
Oh, brother contrite and sincere
Sad regrettable decisions
Rued empty full-on tears

Oh, brother thy guiding star
I listen not to you thine sage
I see you, now I've gone too far
Now that remorse fills my page

Oh, brother for thine an outcast
Thy black sheep who never followed
Much penitence comes belated
Self-pity is all that wallows.

Heart attack

Inflammation sensation
Palpitations somewhere within
Pulse quickened elation
Heartburn begins

Overheated exchanges
Igniting desire
Too hot to handle
One heart on fire
God loves a trier.

Rare

Better late than never
Rarely together
That long wait
Soulmates forever.

Adventures

Reminiscing

Looking back

Nostalgia playing tricks

The good old daze

Dementia!

The worlds end

If the world was to end
Would it restart
With another life
Many worlds apart

For you and I
What lies behind
Unknown territory
That door behind

Clinging to hope
Clinging to each other
The other side
Remains undiscovered.

Clean slate

New me, bitter soul
Filed in the bin
Left behind, my old mind
Along with every sin

My new self
Clean health
Happiness within
Endeavouring to begin.

Sandcastles

Like igloos in the snow
She camouflaged my mind
Bamboozled my demeanour
Entrapment unrefined

Built me up for certain
With her bricks of trust
Then broke me down to rubble
Trampled me into dust

Like sandcastles in the sand
I had no place to hide
Vanishing before morning
I went out with the tide.

July

Pillaging secret July skies
A hush of swallows raping silence
Splashing dives descending dance
A pregnant pause rains on romance
Summer invades
Her screams refrain and fade.

Breakdown

Shattered shards lay splintered eggshells
Threaded cotton darn trodden textiles
Paper trails, stale broken breadcrumbs
A perfect intrusion bluntly succumbs
fumbled at knife point, all fingers and thumbs.

Song for a star

I forgot about the moon
The sunset shut it down
Eclipsing all sad memories
With its amber nectar crown

I forgive the stars
For they did nothing wrong
Glistening in outer space
Listening to your song

I forgive and forget
Almost everything
Except your heavenly body
A reason for me to sing.

Gilt edged

A reverie from my concrete jungle
Summertime's garden of treasure
Reminiscing mother's roses
Remembering fragrant pleasures

The sunshine starts unveiling
Red lilies lost in the mist
Forget me nots that forgot me
Sky’s miniature blue moon kiss

Long shadows continually grow
A definition of dahlias
This picture briefly exposed
Defiantly without failure

A single sunflower is showing
Flowering beyond all reach
Gilded envy of gold petals
Overlooking, she need not peek

My golden globe fast fading
As the sunsets on the lawn
With the jewellery from my daydream
I wear a smile with heartfelt warmth

Shocking

Diving in the cold waters of memories
Plunging into the Icey depths
Tortured recall in total shock
Drowning moments surround deep breaths.

Life and light

Not enough superlatives to describe your worth exist
Your pastel shades create a canvas, sweet calm solace
Vivacious verbs open envied eyes of avarice.
Decanting verse, thirst quenching words, lamented bliss
Surrounding seas glean beautiful skies like amethyst
Infinite smiles with heartfelt sighs now leave these lips.

Waves

Passion

Making waves

Ebbing and flowing

Sometimes coming, sometimes going

Fashion!

Ode to be He wolf *

Fenrir's calling, his ancient forest legacy
Much more than a myth (forget allegedly)
His sacred spirit still prone to attack
This lonely soul once led the pack

A carnivores rise on pernicious intent
Satiating hiraeth deliriously hell bent
Scarred and stretched the ones remained
Nearly Arctic white distemper stained

Primordial howls echo territorial teeth
The legendary boy who cried wolf
Sanctify solidarity since time primeval
Estranged through emotional upheaval

Survival of the fittest, biting and drooling
Opening up old wounds then devouring
Romulus and Remus Capitoline swine
Food for thought, the Canis lupus kind

Under the stars, lay his dominating scent
'Neath tundra aurora' rhyming descent
Scowling strained liberty's endless refrain
Cast melancholy rain on fossilised plain

The sweet parting in the mornings wake
String of nightmares, helmed at fate
transient fur breeds constant with time
Ode to be, He wolf howls in the night

Canine chaos pulchritudinous eyes
Snowing glances shout from his mind
With those cannibalistic rabid stares
The bloodbath lies empty, Fenrir swears.

Embers *

The sound of my beating heart, it speaks
Tones of antagonizing bleakness
Deep within I could never compete
The void of you, dwells incompleteness

Reverberating from the ashes of despair
Painful echoes of romance remembered
My burnt-out heart beyond repair
Your flying kisses in smouldering embers.

Nightingales *

A bush shields a secret passion
Dream land thicket he imagines
Her trills whistling loud
Lifting his blackest clouds,
Chattering her love song bright
She sings day and night

His nightingale hides away
To her tune, sings he'll stay

Did the breeze care for the moon?
Or the night spells wandering plume
On a cloud in his mind
This haze stuck to her rhyme
Her dream catcher in the midst
Weaving gold and amethyst.

As she listened to his calling
His heart rate starts free falling

A soulmate for life flying low
Songbird sorrow, ebb and flow
A nightingale's courtship now displays
Eye to eye's everlasting gaze
At last, they meet their match
Destiny inflames their flight path

Murmuring laden sweet sighs
Embittered days adorn clear skies
Summerly spills before poetic nest
Printing each moment upon each breast
Symmetrical poetry serenading sanity
Amaranthine everlasting symphony.

Flower **

How can I find what is not lost
In waiting for the flower to bloom
To be still no matter the cost
Not let impatience turn to gloom

As becoming is the real joy
Anticipating heightens the gift
Exchanges then will employ
Moments savoured of a first kiss.

Who knows when this will be
Intriguing times lay ahead
I imagine a garden of beauty
From this lonely flowerbed

If becoming became belonging
Then the gift is ours to give
I don’t know where this maybe going
But it gives us a reason to live.

Sky ***

Let me not question thou beauty oh sky
Such wonders that widespread
For the birds flaunt themselves by fly
The magic that it displays
The immense beauty that it portrays
Bringing onto the ray of moonlight
Cherishes the welcome of the night.
The darkness that is space drifts glimpsing stars
Glittering beyond like sunshine rays
Reflecting back as moon dusky scars
A sight for sore eyes way down south
Lost for words but not nil by mouth
Sky is closing as daybreaks again
A vicious circle that can't be tamed.

Eclipsed

Meandering amber porcelain moons
Orbit the Sun's immortal cruise
Searching for words, her eternal eclipse
Lost in a space she could never lose

Far above crushed velvet heavens
Gravitational waves have their say
Such stunning silence of indigo ripples
Hushing echoes mime all the way

High on hopeful Chinese Whispers
Broken promises of intoxicated stars
Her voyage (for sure) way off course
Forever believing, there's life on Mars

Recovering her wishes long eclipsed
Her solar dreams reach one last night
With a final grasp, discovering
Her perfect synchrony of moonlight.

Complicated

Infatuated

Ill-fated

Crossing the line

One more last time

Complicated!

Aura

Humidity, oh the humiliation
Showing humility beyond his patience
Humble is as humble does
Hydrated times, heavens above
Cooling off, heating on
Cometh the ice age
Her ozone, gone!

Sentimental

This fragile parcel
Please handle with care
Destination overseas
Aerial fayre

An irreplaceable load
His reluctant release
One stained glass heart
Her priceless piece.

Heatwave concerto

Ants working hard
Finely tune their hearts
An orchestra of aphids
Suffer for their art

Chittering insects
Too many crickets chirping
Coyotes come a yipping
Doggedly usurping

Baby ballerinas
Dancing in the dark
Leaping and a clinging
Tippy toe starts

A bird calling chorus
Wind whooshing rain
Disharmonious singing
Acapella pain

Playing his piano
Conducted in the shade
Preying in the shadows
A Mantis serenades

Redolent crescendo
Evocative refrain
Encore enamoured
Poignant tears
Again, again and again.

Comfort blanket

Listening to shadows
With one eye open
Anxious about the unknown
Reassuringly hoping

Daydreaming tonight
With closed eyes
Will nightmares stay away
Or come back disguised

Darkness my blanket
Lying on my own
My eyes wide open
Reassuringly alone

Loneliness
It's meant to be
Loneliness
It's meant for me.

Natures blessings

Creation of fascination
(No second guessing)
Biological phenomena
Mother Nature's blessing
In her wonderful world
Essentially caressing

Sensationally touching
Sensitive loving feeling
Both agony and ecstasy
Aesthetically pleasing
Naturally appealing
Fundamentally his breathing

Losing himself he wanders
the seven wonders of the world
Counting his blessings, he wonders
will number eight be his girl?

Abracadabra

I pull the trigger by mistake
Igniting flame
Trickery for beginners
Without smoke and mirrors
Shot down again

Vanishing act – the devil's top hat
Back-to-back pain
Flailing in vain
With my hellfire wand
I cast myself insane.

Wave goodbye

Seaside syllables
Gravitating pulling verse
Tidal wavelength hurt.

Forget me not

Pain healing in time's midst

Fading feelings in the morning mist.

Heightened

Whispered tears hear something's stolen
Goodbyes screaming
My eyes won't open.

Juliet's apple

When Juliet lost thine apple
Ye ugliness did begin
Cleaning up, under protest
Gaining only emptiness
No forgiveness for thy sin

Thou 'twas cut to thy core
Upset ye apple cart
Cometh to no surprise
Hello ye olde goodbye
O'er afore thine start

No fairy tale ending
Only thou art survived
Depressing thine buttons
Returning to thy pumpkin
Cinderella died.

Time bombs

Slipping through Father Time's tight fist
In this void, his impatient abyss
Hanging onto the palm of his hand
Clinging to these clouds, his command
Tension insecurity within
Guessing when the time bombs begin
Sweat dripping, held only by fingertips
Sky high suspense, am I losing my grip?

The black sheep

Children of darkness
Seraphic sanguine blessed
Pulchritudinous!

Rainbows

Mysterious mundane skies
Open their pearly gate eyes
Crying arcane rain
Ethereal silver lined
Esoteric cloud evolution
Nascent to the moribund
Bursting cobalt and azure
Diffractions of the sun.

Full on

Sinful
A skinful of hope
Intoxicated
With Life's optimistic dope
Simple!

What on earth

Humanity! Damn the profanity
I swear, only God knows what it all means
Obsessive obsolete dimensions
Living the dream

The meaning of life
Satisfied merely surviving
Living just to find
Where we go invariably dying

This cursed existence
Persistently breathing
How, when, where and why
Do we go, inexplicably leaving?

Blocked

Anguish
Helplessness
Just a mess
A mind of despair
So unfair
Cannot think
Just one thing
Did you ever really care?
Alone, hurt, tossed
Abandoned
On an island
Lost!
Deserted
Deserving not

This impact

You're too cross

Not knowing

Where to turn

Will I learn?

My heart wrenched

Virtual reality true!

Heartbroken

Will I heal?

Will you return?

Oh God!

Was it a dream?

Blocked forever

So it seems

My lady

My one and only

Funny how
Why you won’t phone me
So many questions
Go round my head
Please end this
Turmoil and dread
I promise you
(Like never before)
To try much harder
Respect you more
I do however
Of that I'm sure
Oh girl
To hear your voice
To hold you tight
To have a choice

That will last

Unless!

You put away the past

(We cannot go on)

Breaking our heart

For we are one

Been through so much

I've said enough!

Over and done.

A world apart

Kicked while he's down
Venus inflicts more pain
Obviously oblivious
As she kicks him again

Repeatedly berating
Deleting easily
Mars, once her world
The defeated enemy

Her rocket lifts off
Alienation achieved
Contented; she looks back
As he can barely breathe

Left devoid without energy
And her engine fully powered
All hope lost to a world
In her ivory tower.

Closure

Closure
Emotional exposure
Over!
Leaving behind
Moving on
Those vulnerable times
Over and done.
As one door closes
Another one opens
Optimism
A way of coping.
No fear
Facing the future
Here's to mine; hoping!

Heaven in her hands****

She deserves all the love offered
To the women of his past
She wants to possess the footsteps
Of all his ups and downs

She wants to belong in his dreams
And his reality
To be his favourite one and only
Deserving everything

Appreciating all he does
She wants to forsake the past
He takes on board her every whim
Says he’s saved the best till last

Behaving more appropriately
Determined to make her sure
Less talk, more seeing his actions
And she'll fall in love once more.

Never trust a poet

When the going gets tough
The rough is scribbled down
Can’t read my own writing
The expression dumfounds

Unmasked worldwide
Written home truths
Minced words versed
Utterly uncouthed
Never trust a poet;

It's as simple as that!

CHAI

Published by kb Independent publishing.com